D0504197

ISBN 0-86163-716-X

Copyright © 1995 Award Publications Limited

First published 1995
Second impression 2002

Published by Award Publications Limited,
27 Longford Street, London NW1 3DZ

Printed in Malaysia

LITTLE OTTER IS MISSING

from Kenneth Grahame's
THE WIND IN THE WILLOWS

Adapted by Jane Carruth

Illustrated by Rene Cloke

AWARD PUBLICATIONS

The Water Rat and Mole had been good friends for a long time and Mole loved the long evenings he spent with his friends—especially in the summer when the days were often fiercely hot and tiring.

Now he was looking for a place where he could stretch out on the bank while Ratty did some fishing in the river.

"I can't do much fishing," the Rat explained, as he settled on a suitable spot. "I've promised Otter a short visit . . ."

"I remember Otter!" Mole cried, as he stretched out on the bank while Ratty waded into the river.

"He came searching for us last winter when you took me to Mr. Badger's house."

By now the Water Rat's little brown paws had a firm hold on his rod and Mole knew that he wasn't likely to want to talk.

"Well, I hope the fish are biting," he said, more to himself than to the Water Rat, and half

closed his eyes. It was a shame Ratty had to go to Otter's place but it probably wouldn't take long and afterwards there would be time to talk about the day's adventures.

Mole was nearly asleep when the Water Rat came to tell him the fish weren't rising and he was going to visit Otter.

"Otter's place isn't far from here," he said. "I'll have a word with him and see how Little Portly is getting on . . ."

"Little Portly? Oh, you mean baby Otter!" Mole murmured sleepily. "I know!"

8

The Water Rat was as good as his word.
He came back much sooner than Mole expected.

"I tell you, Mole," he exclaimed,
as he settled down beside him on the
bank, "I couldn't have stayed any longer with
Otter—even if I had wanted to. He's in a
dreadful state . . ."

The Water Rat seemed so upset that Mole sat up
and did his best to look intelligent. "What on
earth has happened?" he asked. "It's so lovely
here and peaceful—surely nothing too awful?"

Ratty put a brown paw on Mole's arm and
murmured, "I know we planned a peaceful evening
but that's out of the question now. Little

Otter is missing and his father is nearly out of his mind with worry. He was just going out again to look for him. You know what he thinks about Little Portly even though he is always playing about and chasing silly things—like butterflies!''

"What does Otter think can have happened to him?" Mole asked lightly. "Everybody round here knows him so he's not likely to come to much harm."

"Well, he's been missing for some days now," said the Rat seriously. "And Father Otter is afraid of the water-mill for one thing. He says Little Otter can't swim very well . . ."

12

Mole was silent for some time. Then he said in quite a different voice, "I tell you what, Ratty, you go back to Otter and offer him our help tonight. We know the river and we're on good terms with all the animals . . ."

The Water Rat looked relieved at Mole's suggestion. "I'll go now," he said, getting to his feet. "I won't waste time."

The Rat found Otter looking more miserable than ever. "It's no use worrying, Otter," he said cheerfully. "Both Mole and I have made up our minds to search all night. In fact we won't go home until we find him . . ."

As soon as Ratty joined Mole again he said, "Mole, we'll get out the boat and paddle up stream. I've promised Otter we won't go home until we find him."

"Just what I was thinking," said Mole. "Let's go!" They hurried back to the house and with Mole's help the Water Rat got his boat out.

"The night is half-gone already," the Water Rat said. "But we may pick up some news of him as we go along."

14

After some argument, it was agreed that the
Rat should take the oars and Mole take charge
of the steering.

The night was full of small noises and the
two friends were afraid to speak in case they
missed some important sound which would help
them in their search.

"Otter is spending the night by the old ford,"
Ratty said at last. "That's where he gave

Little Otter his first swimming lesson and where
he caught his first fish . . .". He broke off, as
Mole suddenly stopped steering and whispered,
"Did—did you hear something—something we
don't usually hear?"

They waited. Then the
moon lifted and they began
to recognise some of their
old friends on the river
bank. As it steadily grew
lighter they fastened their
boat to a willow and the
Rat said, "Let's leave it
here for a time."

17

Slowly and patiently the
two friends began to explore
the hedges, the hollow trees
and the ditches. Mole soon
grew weary of the search.

But the Water Rat was tireless. Up and down
he went—not leaving a stone unturned. He
even peered into tree-hollows which were far
too small to shelter a baby otter.

Mole said as much and Rat remarked finally,
"Oh, very well, let's get in the boat again and
work our way up the stream."

The fields and trees became clearer and a
light breeze sprang up and rustled the reeds
and bulrushes. Somewhere a bird piped suddenly
and Ratty stood up in the boat and begged
his friend to listen.

Mole, who had been keeping the boat moving with gentle strokes, turned his head in the direction the Water Rat was pointing.

He listened for a moment. Then he said, "I don't hear anything special, Ratty. Just the wind in the rushes . . ."

The Rat sighed. "It was special!"

After a moment the Rat sank back in the boat. "It's gone!" he whispered.

"What was it like?" Mole asked, as he kept the boat moving gently forward.

"Like—like the sweet clear sound of piping," Ratty said softly. "The music seemed to be calling us. Row on, Mole, row on."

Mole obeyed and the light grew steadily stronger. Then suddenly, there it was—a tiny green island, bordered with flowers.

The two friends, without a word, moored their boat and landed, pushing their way through low, scented bushes and tall grasses, until the Rat whispered, "Stop! Listen!"

"What is it, Ratty?" Mole asked. Then he turned in the direction Ratty was looking. "It's the piping, isn't it?
Can you hear the piping?"

"Let's go," Rat said. "We can't turn back now. The music is calling us!" He plunged forward and Mole followed. They did not stop until they came to tall reeds and rushes which the Water Rat impatiently pushed aside.

Suddenly Mole felt a great awe. He bowed
his head as if he were in the presence of some
mighty king. His feet seemed rooted to the
ground. With difficulty he turned to look at
his friend and saw that Ratty was trembling.

"Rat," he whispered, "are you afraid?"

"No, not really," Rat whispered back. "I
know about him, you see. It's the god Pan.
His wonderful music comes from a pipe made of
reeds and he rules over the forests and the
fields and the . . ."

"And the animals," Mole said. "Look! He's
got Little Otter fast asleep beside him."

With a cry of delight the Rat ran
towards the sleeping baby Otter.

Mole stood still for a moment. It was as if he was wakening from a beautiful dream. But he couldn't call out to Ratty who had suddenly stopped in his tracks, his eyes shining in his brown face, as he peered at the ground.

The air was now full of bird song and Mole shook his head. Dawn was breaking but of the smiling god Pan there was no sign. He had vanished. It was as if he had never been!

The baby Otter woke up with a happy squeak and wriggled with pleasure when he saw his father's two friends.

"Come on, Ratty," Mole called. "Help me get the little fellow into the boat . . ."

But the Rat did not come immediately. He was still staring down at some hoof-marks. "Some animal—or Pan himself, half-god and half-animal has made these," he told himself, before going to help his friend lift baby Otter into the boat. "What a night this has been!"

The sun was up as the friends paddled off.

Little Otter was now placed securely at the bottom of the boat. But as they drew near the familiar ford, there was father Otter, and they lifted Little Otter out when the boat was steered into the bank. They waited, sharing Otter's joy, as the baby broke into a clumsy waddle at the sight of Otter. And they smiled at each other when they heard Otter's amazed, happy bark as he greeted his missing Little Otter.

"I feel strangely tired, Rat,"
said Mole as they set out for home.
"So do I," murmured Rat dreamily.
"But it's been a wonderful night . . ."
Then the weary Rat closed his eyes
and fell fast asleep.